THE GAMER

MUSIC MONSTER!

by Shawn Pryor
illustrated by Francesca Ficorilli

raintree
a Capstone company — publishers for children

Raintree is an imprint of Capstone Global Library Limited, a company
incorporated in England and Wales having its registered office at 264
Banbury Road, Oxford, OX2 7DY – Registered company number: 6695582

www.raintree.co.uk
myorders@raintree.co.uk

Edited by Aaron Sautter
Designed by Brann Garvey
Original illustrations © Capstone Global Library Limited 2023
Originated by Capstone Global Library Ltd

978 1 3982 4909 7

British Library Cataloguing in Publication Data
A full catalogue record for this book is available from the British Library.

CONTENTS

You may believe that video games and apps are just harmless fun. But in these special places where we play, a hero works to protect us from the dangers that exist in those worlds . . .

Meet **THE GAMER**, defender of Earth and the digital realm!

REAL NAME: Tyler Morant

HERO NAME: The Gamer

AGE: 13

HERO TOOL: Gamer Activation
Device, which transforms
Tyler into the Gamer

ENEMY: Cynthia Cyber

MISSION: To defeat evil Cynthia Cyber
and her wicked digital monsters

CHAPTER ONE

THE TERRORHORN AWAKES!

Tyler is enjoying the outdoor music **festival** at the city park.

"I'm glad I don't have to be a superhero today," Tyler says. "I can't wait to hear my cousin Marty play."

Moments later Marty and his band step on the stage. The crowd **cheers**!

"Show them what you've got, Marty!" Tyler yells.

The band begins to play, and Marty puts his trumpet to his lips. But just as he blows into the horn, a **laser** beam zaps it!

The trumpet starts to **glow** and makes weird noises.

Everyone in the crowd covers their ears.

"This sounds awful!" someone in the crowd says.

Marty drops the blaring trumpet as it glows **red hot**.

"This doesn't look good at all. Marty, get the band off the stage, now!" Tyler yells.

The band jumps off stage as the trumpet grows into a **giant spider-like monster**!

"Finally, I'm free! Cynthia Cyber's monster ray worked!" the monster shouts.

"Marty, can you and your band get everyone out of here safely?" asks Tyler.

Marty nods his head. "We're on it. Let's go!"

Tyler looks on as the crowd flees the festival. "Okay, monster, it's just you and me."

The monster just laughs. "No one can stop **TERRORHORN**. It's time for you to blow away!"

The Terrorhorn starts to blow . . .

FrEEEOooooooooo!!

The noise and powerful **blast** of wind sends Tyler flying!

WHOOSH!

Tyler thinks quickly as he flies through the air. *I need to stop this* **menace** *before it blows the city to pieces.*

"GAMER, TRANSFORM!"

CHAPTER TWO

SOUNDS LIKE TROUBLE

Tyler transforms into the Gamer and lands safely on the ground.

"You've caused enough trouble, trumpet!" the Gamer says, holding his Energy Sword.

The beast begins to grow even bigger than before. Its trumpet-shaped snout starts to glow.

"I've only begun my destruction. After I **defeat** you, I'll blow your entire city to rubble!" the trumpet beast screams.

The Gamer **charges** towards the monster. "Not if I stop you first!"

The hero and the monster clash . . .

Terrorhorn blocks the Gamer's Energy Sword with its huge horn. Then it swats the hero with a mighty blow.

The Gamer tumbles and bounces across the ground. He finally **crashes** into a tree.

Whoa! This evil trumpet packs a punch!

As the Gamer stands up, he hears a familiar noise.

FrEEEOooooooo!!

Terrorhorn's **blast** blows the Gamer across the park, and he lands in the city pool.

WHOOSH!

SPLASH!

Woozy from the blast, the Gamer stands up shakily. Then he sees a lot of families around the pool looking at him.

"Everybody, get out of here! There's a monster coming – GO!"

The people leave the pool quickly as the trumpet monster arrives.

"I thought that blast would've finished you!" Terrorhorn yells. "No problem. That just means I get more chances to **smash** you to bits."

CHAPTER THREE

WET INSTRUMENTS

The Gamer taps a button on his wrist pad. "Where did Cynthia find this monster? And how can I stop it?" he asks.

The Gamer's wrist pad answers, "Cynthia used a **transformation** ray. It turned the trumpet into a **monster**."

"Terrorhorn is from the game *Record Wreckers*," the wrist pad continues. "Searching for a solution to beat it."

Suddenly, Terrorhorn **charges** towards the Gamer.

I have to slow him down while my wrist pad finds an answer, the hero thinks.

"I'm going to squash you flat!" says the charging trumpet beast.

The Gamer quickly finds a large beach ball. He picks it up and throws it at Terrorhorn's feet. The monster trips and **stumbles** to the ground.

The Gamer then grabs the beach ball
and **shoves** it into the monster trumpet's
big mouth.

"MMMPH-MMMPH-MMMPH!"

Terrorhorn mumbles, not able to talk.

The Gamer then shoves the monster, and it falls backwards into the pool.

SPLASH!

CRASH!

"Looks like you're all wet, Terrorhorn!" the Gamer says.

But suddenly the water level in the pool starts to drop. It's like someone is **drinking** the pool water with a straw.

"Oh no, the trumpet beast is draining the pool!" the Gamer exclaims.

Then Terrorhorn fires a huge **blast** of water at the hero.

The blast sends the Gamer flying through the air!

CHAPTER FOUR

FINDING A FREQUENCY

With a **thundering** boom, the Gamer crashes into a park fountain.

"Uugh . . . I guess I'm the one who's wet," says the Gamer. "That blast really hurt!"

The Gamer's wrist pad alerts him.

"To defeat Terrorhorn, you need a musical **instrument** that can cancel his battle blast."

"What kind of instrument?" asks the Gamer.

"An electric guitar," the wrist pad replies.

A worker in a nearby music shop runs over to the Gamer. "Are you okay?" the worker says.

"I have a monster trumpet to defeat," the Gamer says. "Do you have an electric guitar I can use?"

"We do!" says the worker. "Stay here. I'll be right back."

The worker **dashes** to the shop and grabs a red electric guitar. He quickly brings it to the Gamer.

"Scanning guitar . . . prepare for **upgrade**," says the Gamer's wrist pad.

"ENERGIZE!!!!!" yells the Gamer.

The Gamer starts to **glow** with energy. His **armour** changes. Speakers are added to his suit and the guitar is transformed into a **laser rifle**.

"I promise to bring the guitar back when I'm done!" the Gamer says.

CHAPTER FIVE

MUSICAL MAYHEM!

FrEEEOoooooooo!!

Terrorhorn has grown to giant size! He blows his horn. The loud sounds **shake** and **crack** buildings. The people run in fear.

"Where are you, Gamer? Are you **scared** to face me?"

The upgraded Gamer suddenly appears before Terrorhorn. "I'm **never** afraid of Cynthia Cyber's monsters!"

"We'll see about that," says the trumpet beast. Then he begins to blow!

"**Rock Star Armour, activate**!" shouts the Gamer.

The speakers from the Gamer's armour begin making noise.

The Gamer's power speakers **cancel** Terrorhorn's blast.

"You stopped my noise blast! How did
you do that?" yells Terrorhorn.

"It's a secret," says the Gamer. Then he aims his laser guitar rifle at the monster. **"Rock Star Super Blast, FIRE!"**

A large, musical-note shaped laser blast fires from the Gamer's rifle.

The laser blast hits Terrorhorn, and the monster **explodes**!

Terrorhorn is **defeated**!

All that remains is Marty's trumpet. It's returned to normal size.

"Awesome, I'm giving this back to Marty," says the Gamer, picking up the instrument. "The concert is back on!"

GLOSSARY

activate start up or turn something on

armour hard, protective covering for the body

defeat beat someone in a battle or contest

festival celebration that often features musical groups or artistic events

instrument device used to make music

laser narrow, powerful ray of light

menace someone whose actions are dangerous or harmful

transformation change from one form to another

upgrade improve something

TALK ABOUT IT

1. The Gamer uses an electric guitar to upgrade his power suit. What would've happened if he had used a different instrument?

2. The Gamer had different powers after he was upgraded. How did his new powers help to defeat Terrorhorn?

WRITE ABOUT IT

1. In this story, Terrorhorn used loud noise and wind to battle the Gamer. If you were a musical instrument monster, what kind would you be? Write a paragraph explaining your powers and how they work.

2. The Gamer defeats Terrorhorn. But what happens to his cousin Marty and the band? Do they help get people to safety? Write a story about what Marty does to help protect people at the festival.

THE AUTHOR

Shawn Pryor is the creator and co-author of the graphic novel mystery series Cash and Carrie, co-creator and author of the 2019 Glyph-nominated football/drama series Force and author of *Kentucky Kaiju* and *Diamond Double Play*, from Jake Maddox Sports Stories. In his free time, he enjoys reading, cooking, listening to streaming music playlists and talking about why Zack from *Mighty Morphin Power Rangers* is the greatest superhero of all time.

THE ILLUSTRATOR

Francesca Ficorilli was born and lives in Rome, Italy. Francesca knew that she wanted to be an artist when she was a child. She was encouraged by her love for animation and her mother's passion for fine arts. After earning a degree in animation, Francesca started working as a freelance animator and illustrator. She finds inspirations for her illustrations in every corner of the world.